Bubble and

"This is their last chance, Mary," Mr Connor said sternly. "If the pups can't keep themselves clean, they really will have to live outside in a kennel. And they won't be allowed into the house at all."

Bubble and Squeak looked at each other and whimpered. They didn't want to live in a horrible old kennel.

As Mary went off to fill the outhouse sink with water, Squeak yapped at his brother, "Bubble, we've just *got* to keep clean from now on . . ."

Titles in Jenny Dale's PUPPY TALES™ series

All of Jenny Dale's PUPPY TALES books can
be ordered at your local bookshop or are
available by post from Book Service by Post
(tel: 01624 675137)

Bubble and Squeak

by Jenny Dale

Illustrated by Susan Hellard

A Working Partners Book

MACMILLAN CHILDREN'S BOOKS

To the real Mary Connor – a true friend

Special thanks to Narinder Dhami

First published 2001 by Macmillan Children's Books
a division of Macmillan Publishers Limited
25 Eccleston Place, London SW1W 9NF
Basingstoke and Oxford
www.macmillan.com

Associated companies throughout the world

Created by Working Partners Limited
London W6 0QT

ISBN 0 330 48369 2

3 5 7 9 8 6 4

A CIP catalogue record for this book is available from
the British Library.

Typeset by SX Composing DTP, Rayleigh, Essex
Printed and bound in Great Britain by Mackays of Chatham plc, Kent

Chapter One

"Come on, Squeak!" Bubble barked, as he splashed about in the foamy bubbles. "The water's lovely!"

"I don't want a bath," Squeak whined, his ears flat against his head. He backed into a corner and tried to make himself as small as possible.

"Look at the pair of you – you're both filthy." Mary Connor, the pups' owner, was pouring dog shampoo over Bubble's muddy back. "You look more like two brown dogs than two white ones!"

"We were only playing, Mary," Bubble woofed, snapping at a bubble that floated up into the air. "We rolled in the mud, and we had a *great* time!"

"But now we've got to have another horrible *bath*," Squeak whimpered. Miserably, he plumped down on his fat little bottom and put his head on his paws. It was all right for Bubble – he loved baths. Squeak hated them even more than he hated going to the vet!

"I hope I can get you both clean before Dad sees you," Mary said, looking worried. She lifted Bubble out and began to dry him with an old towel.

"Yes, Squeak, we don't want Mr Connor to see that we've got dirty *again*," Bubble yapped anxiously. "You know he doesn't like it."

Squeak's heart sank. He knew Bubble was right. He'd have to have a bath, or Mr Connor would be cross. Mary's dad didn't think Bubble and Squeak were the right sort of dogs to live on a busy farm. Until a few weeks ago, the puppy twins had lived in a house with their mum, Molly, and her owner, Mr Nolan. Then Mary had

arrived to collect them with her
mum and dad . . .

"Oh, they're gorgeous!" Mary
said.

Bubble and Squeak rushed over
to meet her, their tails wagging.
Mary's voice was soft, and she
handled the pups gently when
she stroked them.

"She's nice!" Squeak woofed.

"I like her!" Bubble barked.

Mrs Connor looked nice too.

But Mr Connor stood there frowning. "They're *white*," he said. "I thought they'd be brown, like Molly."

Mr Nolan shrugged. "Well, they're the only ones left from the litter."

Bubble and Squeak looked at each other, then crept away to hide behind their mum. They weren't sure why Mr Connor didn't like their white coats.

"With all the rain and mud they'll be filthy the whole time," Mr Connor went on.

"Oh, Dad," Mary said. She picked the pups up, hugging one in each arm. "I'll keep them clean.

I'll bath them whenever they need it!"

"Bath?" Squeak gave a puzzled woof. "What's that?"

"They *are* very cute, John," Mary's mum added.

Mr Connor sighed, and nodded his head.

"Thanks, Dad!" Mary cried. She rushed over to kiss him, still carrying the two pups . . .

The trouble was, Mr Connor was right, Squeak thought. It *was* difficult for him and his brother to stay clean on the farm. There were just too many tempting puddles and muddy fields and damp ditches!

And when they got muddy,

Mary had to bath them in the big outhouse sink before they were allowed into the kitchen.

"Come on, Squeak," Mary said, as she finished drying Bubble. "It's your turn now."

"No-o-o-o!" Squeak howled as Mary bent to pick him up.

Just then, the outhouse door opened. Squeak's eyes lit up. This was his chance! He wriggled away from Mary, and made a dash for it.

Mary and Bubble jumped up to chase after him, and Mary knocked the soapdish flying.

"Oh no, you don't, Squeak!" A firm hand grasped the scruff of Squeak's neck, just as he reached the doorway. "Here's the little rascal, Mary." Mr Connor handed a whimpering Squeak over to his daughter. "And make sure he doesn't get away this time – aaargh!"

Mary's dad slipped on the bar of soap, which had fallen to the floor. He skidded forward, and went head-first into the sink full of bubbles.

Chapter Two

Mr Connor wiped the suds from
his face. "I *knew* these two pups
would be trouble!" he shouted
crossly.

"Sorry, Dad!" Mary cried. "I
knocked the soapdish over when
Squeak escaped."

"Well, either they keep clean

from now on, or they'll have to live outside – and I mean it this time!" Mr Connor stomped off across the farmyard.

Squeak looked at Bubble in dismay. Mr Connor sounded really serious. And now Mary was in trouble too. "OK, I'll have a bath now," he whimpered. "But we'd better not get mucky tomorrow."

"What shall we do today then, Bubble?" Squeak yapped.

It was the following morning. Mary was eating breakfast before going to school. The puppies were waiting hopefully for titbits under the kitchen table.

"We could chase the ducks

around the farmyard," Bubble woofed, wagging his tail cheerfully. "And then we could go into the field and find some lovely cowpats to roll in. And then we could find a big puddle and—"

"No, no, *no*!" Squeak barked. "You heard what Mr Connor said. He'll make us live outside if we get dirty again so soon."

"But we're dogs – and dogs *like* getting dirty," Bubble pointed out.

"I know." Squeak nipped his brother's ear playfully. "But Mr Connor doesn't like it."

"So?" Bubble jumped on Squeak. "Mr Connor isn't very clean himself after he's worked on the farm all day, is he? He stinks!"

11

"But at least Mr Connor likes having baths," Squeak panted, as he and Bubble rolled over and over underneath the table. "*I* don't! So let's try and keep clean from now on," he growled, pinning Bubble to the ground.

"What are those two up to?" Mr Connor peered under the table.

"They're just playing, Dad," Mary laughed, as the two pups sat up and shook themselves.

"Would you hurry up, Mary, and finish your breakfast, please?" Mrs Connor said. "You too, John."

"But, Bridie, I've only just sat down to my bacon and eggs!" Mary's dad said grumpily.

"Well, I have to get on with the cleaning, John," said Mrs Connor. "This house is a terrible mess."

Mary and her father looked at each other. "Mrs Riley!" they groaned.

Mary's mum looked flustered. "Well, yes, Mrs Riley *is* coming to visit this afternoon."

"Great! Mrs Riley!" Bubble woofed. "She brought a yummy cake last time, and dropped lots of crumbs!"

"I remember!" Squeak woofed back. "I wonder what she'll bring this time?"

"Not that woman again," Mary's dad grumbled. "All she does is boast about how much money she's got."

"And she's really snooty too," Mary added, slipping two bits of toast under the table.

"Hey, you nicked the biggest bit!" Bubble yapped, as Squeak wolfed it down.

"Well, she *is* a neighbour," Mrs Connor muttered. She began to wipe the kitchen table.

"Can I finish my breakfast before you wipe my plate?" Mary's dad said, as Mrs Connor picked up his plate of bacon and eggs and wiped the table underneath it.

"Mum, will you keep Bubble and Squeak inside today, please?" Mary asked. She picked up her schoolbag. "I don't want them getting dirty again."

"Yes, but they'd better not get under my feet," Mrs Connor said. "I'm going to be very busy."

"I don't want to stay inside," Squeak whined as he and Bubble went to see Mary safely out of the house, as they did every morning.

"Bye, Bubble. Bye, Squeak." Mary kissed each pup in turn. "Be good!"

"At least we'll keep clean if we stay inside, Squeak," Bubble pointed out.

Squeak wagged his tail more cheerfully. "That's true."

"And there are loads of games we can play inside," Bubble woofed. "Come on, let's go and play *Hide-Mr-Connor's-slippers*!"

The pups raced each other up

the stairs.

But Mrs Connor had got there before them, and was dusting the bedroom furniture. "Out!" she said crossly.

Bubble and Squeak whined as Mrs Connor shut the door, leaving them on the landing.

"I know," Squeak barked. "Let's go and play *Hide-under-Mary's-rug!*"

That was one of their favourite games. One of the pups would crawl under the rug on Mary's bedroom floor, while the other one pounced on him every time he moved. It was great fun.

But not for long. The pups had hardly started their game before Mrs Connor bustled in with her duster.

"Out you go!" she said briskly.

"It's not fair!" Squeak complained, but Mrs Connor put them outside, and closed the door *again*.

It was the same all morning. Whenever the pups tried to play a quiet game of *Chew-the-bathmat* or *Running-up-and-down-the-stairs-very-fast*, Mrs Connor put a stop to it.

"We can't do *anything*," Squeak whined as they sat in the hall. They'd been shut out of every single room in the farmhouse.

"Well, maybe we could *help* Mrs Connor instead of playing games," Bubble woofed. "Look!"

Mrs Connor was battling with some kind of monster which had been hiding in the cupboard under the stairs. Bubble and Squeak both growled and bared their teeth. She would *definitely* need their help now. It was their duty to protect Mary and her family from this big, noisy monster!

"Grrr! We're ready for you!" Bubble barked. He dashed down the hall towards Mrs Connor. "I'll bark at you until you stop making that horrible noise!"

"And I'll bite you!" Squeak growled. He grabbed one end of the monster and hung onto it as Mrs Connor tried to push it along.

"Right, that's it! I can't even hoover in peace," Mrs Connor said crossly. She stormed over to the back door and opened it. "Outside – NOW!"

The pups trailed gloomily out into the farmyard.

"Doesn't Mrs Connor know we're trying to help?" Bubble yapped, as he sniffed the air. It had been raining, and everything smelled cool and damp.

"Remember what we said about keeping clean, Bubble!" Squeak

woofed anxiously. The farmyard was awash with mud, and there were lots of puddles.

"Oh, yes . . ." Bubble's eyes lit up. He'd noticed a really *big* puddle, right next to them.

"We don't want to live outside in a kennel, do we?" Squeak reminded him.

"No," Bubble agreed. But the puddle looked so deep, he just *had* to jump right into the middle of it – and he splashed Squeak from head to toe.

"You did that on purpose!" Squeak whined as Bubble ran off, barking gleefully.

Squeak chased his brother through every puddle in the farmyard. Soon, both pups were soaked and filthy. They headed off into one of the fields, where Bubble found some even thicker mud to roll around in. It had been churned up by Mr Connor's tractor.

"I'm hungry!" Squeak whined when they were covered in mud from head to toe.

"So am I," woofed Bubble. He headed back to the farmhouse. Squeak followed.

As usual, the back door was propped open. The two pups charged into the kitchen, leaving muddy pawprints on the clean floor.

Bubble stopped and sniffed the air. "I can smell someone different," he yapped. "Mrs Riley must be here!"

Squeak didn't reply. He was too busy stealing a dog biscuit from Bubble's bowl.

"Hey, I was saving that for later," Bubble barked crossly. Squeak took to his heels, still carrying the biscuit in his mouth, and headed for the living room.

A woman in posh clothes sat on the sofa next to Mrs Connor. It was Mrs Riley. She looked around the room and sniffed snootily. "It must be *very* difficult, trying to keep things clean on a farm," she said. "I do feel sorry for you, Bridie."

Mrs Connor went a bit red. "Oh, it's not too bad," she said.

Mrs Riley looked at Mary's mum. "You should see *my* house," she said. "It's spotless. But then, of course, I *do* have a cleaner and a housekeeper."

"More tea?" Mrs Connor asked grumpily, picking up the tea tray. "I'll just pop out to the kitchen and put the kettle on again."

Right at that moment Squeak barged into the living room, followed by Bubble. Mrs Connor was just behind the door, and the tray was knocked right out of her hands.

"Oh!" Mrs Connor gasped as everything crashed to the floor.

Bubble and Squeak didn't even notice. They were too busy greeting the visitor.

"Have you brought anything nice to eat?" Bubble barked. "That

cake you brought last time was yummy!" He jumped up at Mrs Riley and left muddy pawprints all over her cream skirt.

"I bet there's something nice in here!" Squeak yapped. He stuck his nose into Mrs Riley's big shiny handbag. He was so excited, he dropped the dog biscuit inside it.

"Help!" Mrs Riley screamed. "Get these filthy little dogs away from me!"

Chapter Three

"It was your fault for jumping in that puddle, Squeak!" Bubble whined.

"No, it was *yours* for finding all that lovely mud to roll in!" Squeak whimpered.

The puppies were in disgrace.

Mrs Riley had stormed out of

the farmhouse, and Mary's mum had had to clean up all the mess. But first she'd shut the pups in an empty pig-pen.

"And you can stay there till Mary comes home from school!" Mrs Connor had said crossly, slamming the door shut.

Bubble and Squeak huddled together in a corner of the smelly pen, feeling very worried. What would Mary say when she saw them? What would Mr Connor say?

"Don't worry, Squeak." Bubble licked his brother's nose. "Mary will give us a bath, and everything will be OK."

"*Another* bath," Squeak whined. He shivered.

Suddenly Bubble sat up and sniffed the air. "It's Mary!" he barked.

A moment later, Mary popped her head over the side of the pen. "Look at you two!" she said. "You're both filthy, and Mum's really angry."

Bubble and Squeak huddled together sadly, their stumpy tails between their legs.

Mary sighed, shaking her head. Then she let herself into the pen and picked them both up for a cuddle.

Bubble licked her ear. "We're very sorry, Mary," he woofed softly.

"At least *you* don't mind if we're dirty or not," Squeak whimpered as he snuffled his nose into Mary's neck.

Mr and Mrs Connor came out into the farmyard. They both looked furious. Bubble and Squeak's hearts sank.

"Put those pups down, Mary!" Mrs Connor said sharply. "You'll get your school clothes dirty."

Mary quickly put Bubble and Squeak down on the ground. "I'm really sorry about what happened, Mum," she said.

"I've never been so embarrassed in my life," Mrs Connor went on. "And in front of Mrs Riley too."

"This is their last chance, Mary," Mr Connor said sternly. "If the pups can't keep themselves clean, they really will have to live outside in a kennel. And they won't be allowed in the house at all. I've had enough."

Bubble and Squeak looked at each other and whimpered. They didn't want to live in a horrible old kennel. They wanted to be with Mary in the farmhouse. They wanted to sleep on Mary's bed. And sit under the kitchen table waiting for titbits. And curl up in front of the fire in the living room – like they always did.

As Mary went off to fill the outhouse sink with water, Squeak yapped at his brother. "Bubble, we've just *got* to keep clean from now on."

"I know," Bubble yapped in

agreement. "Don't worry, it'll be easy!"

But it *wasn't* easy. It rained a lot – and that made the farmyard even muddier. Mary helped all she could. When she took Bubble and Squeak out for their morning walk, she carried them over the muddiest puddles. But she couldn't help when she was at school.

"Mind that puddle, Squeak!" Bubble barked, as they took a stroll around the farmyard the following afternoon.

Squeak tiptoed carefully round it. He couldn't help staring at the puddle as he did so. He was longing to jump in and splash around. But he knew Mary would be upset, so he didn't.

"Yaaah! Can't catch me!" One of the ducks scurried past on its way to the pond, quacking loudly.

Bubble was about to chase after it when Squeak grabbed his tail.

"No, Bubble!" he barked. "Look at the mud around the pond!"

Bubble growled a bit, then gave up on the duck-chasing idea.

The two pups raced back into the farmhouse, where it was a lot safer.

At least, they *thought* they were safe.

While Bubble was sniffing around the big open fireplace, a shower of soot fell down the chimney. It nearly covered him in black dust. Luckily, Bubble jumped out of the way, just in time.

"We can't go *anywhere* or do *anything*!" Squeak yapped. "There's dirt all over the place!"

"But just think how happy Mary will be that we're still white!" Bubble barked.

And he was right. Mary was

really pleased when she came home from school and saw her two clean puppies. "Well done, boys!" she cried, giving them both a hug.

But Bubble and Squeak couldn't help feeling worried. This was only the first day, and it had been *really* difficult. How on earth were they going to keep it up?

Chapter Four

"Bubble and Squeak have been very good, haven't they, Mum?" Mary asked proudly.

She was sitting with her mum in the living room, watching TV. The pups were curled up together in one big fluffy white ball on her lap. "They've stayed clean for a whole week."

"And it was really difficult too," Bubble yapped.

"But at least it means no baths!" Squeak woofed.

The pups had spent most of their time playing and sleeping in Mary's bedroom, where they felt safe. It was very boring staying inside all the time, but at least they hadn't got dirty.

Mrs Connor put her knitting down as the programme finished, and the adverts began. "Well, let's hope it lasts," she said. "I'll go and put the kettle on. Your dad should be home from the market soon."

"I bet you're the first one to get dirty!" Squeak yapped. He gave his brother a little nip.

"No, I bet *you* are!" Bubble nipped him back, and they started rolling around together on Mary's lap.

"New Kleener-than-Kleen's wonderful *bubbles* will make your hair *squeaky* clean!" said a loud voice.

Bubble and Squeak stopped rolling around and sat up, their ears pricked.

"Someone said our names!" Bubble barked.

"Who was it?" Squeak yapped.

Mary was laughing. "Look, Mum!" she said, as Mrs Connor paused in the doorway. "The pups heard their names on the TV!"

Bubble and Squeak knew what

the TV was. It was that strange box in the corner of the room that had lots of people and sometimes even other dogs inside it. They stared at the screen.

A woman was shaking her long hair around, and holding a big green bottle. "It's true!" she said. "*Kleener-than-Kleen*'s bubbles really *do* make your hair squeaky clean!"

Bubble and Squeak began to bark when they heard their names again. "She's talking about us!"

Mary grinned. "Maybe we should get some *Kleener-than-Kleen* shampoo for Bubble and Squeak!" she joked. "Not that they need it," she added quickly, as her mum frowned. "They're being so good at the moment. They're already cleaner-than-clean!"

Bubble and Squeak looked at each other proudly. They were cleaner-than-clean! That wasn't bad for two pups who had been in trouble for being filthy just a week ago. Now all they had to do was keep it up . . .

"I hope you boys are going to be

careful," Mrs Connor said with a frown. She was pegging out some washing, a few days later. The sun had come out – but it had been raining for hours and hours, and the farmyard was full of muddy puddles.

"Of *course* we're going to be careful!" Bubble sniffed, as Mrs Connor picked up the washing-basket and went inside.

"What shall we do now?" Squeak woofed.

"Let's wait by the gate for Mary to come home from school," Bubble yapped back.

"OK," Squeak agreed.

But as they were making their way over to the gate, something happened. A huge gust of wind blew across the farmyard. It tugged a yellow T-shirt off the washing-line and carried it away.

Bubble didn't notice, but Squeak did. "Oh no!" he barked. "That's Mary's favourite T-shirt!"

Determined to get the T-shirt back, Squeak chased after it. Splash! He ran through one muddy puddle. Splash! And another.

"Squeak! Be careful!" Bubble yelped, horrified.

Suddenly the wind died down for a moment and the T-shirt fell to the ground.

Squeak rushed towards it through the mud. He grabbed it in his teeth. "Goth ith!" he woofed. It was hard to woof with T-shirt in his mouth.

"And the mud's got *you*!" Bubble whined, rushing over to him. "Squeak, you're *filthy*!"

Chapter Five

Squeak looked down at himself. He *was* dirty. In fact, he was dirtier-than-dirty! He dropped the T-shirt back on the ground. "Bubble, what are we going to do?" he whimpered. "If Mr and Mrs Connor see me like this, we'll never be allowed in the house again."

"And Mary will be really upset," Bubble added. Then his ears perked up and his tail started to wag. "I've got a brilliant idea!"

Squeak's ears perked up too. "What?" he asked.

"*I'll* bath you!" Bubble barked.

"Oh no!" Squeak lay his ears flat against his head and backed away from his brother. "No way!" he woofed.

"Have you got any better ideas?" Bubble yapped sternly.

Squeak looked glum. "No," he sniffed.

"Come on, then," Bubble woofed. He turned and headed off towards the stables on the other side of the farmyard.

Squeak picked up Mary's T-shirt

and followed his brother.

"We can't bath you in the outhouse sink," Bubble woofed as he ran, "because we can't turn the taps on. But I know where there is some water already poured."

He stopped by one of the troughs that were full of drinking water for the horses. "You'll have to have a bath in there!"

Squeak dropped the T-shirt again,

then howled. "But that's for the *horses*. And anyway, you can't bath me – you haven't got any soap!"

Bubble cocked his head to one side. "You're right, Squeak," he woofed. "I'll go and get some." He dashed off towards the house.

Mrs Connor was on the phone when Bubble sneaked in, so she didn't see him run up the stairs into the bathroom.

Panting, Bubble stopped and looked around. He couldn't see the doggy soap Mary always used when she bathed them. But there was a big green bottle on the side of the bath. Bubble had seen that same bottle on the TV. It was *Kleener-than-Kleen*! Mrs Connor must have bought it when she went shopping the day before.

Perfect, Bubble thought. He grabbed the bottle in his teeth, and hurried outside again.

Squeak was waiting by the horse trough, shivering.

Bubble dropped the bottle on the ground. "Help me get the top off, Squeak," he yapped.

First Squeak tucked Mary's T-shirt safely under the trough where it couldn't blow away again. Then Bubble held the bottle between his paws while Squeak twisted the top off with his teeth.

"In you get, Squeak," Bubble yapped firmly after he'd tipped a drop of shampoo into the trough.

"Do I *have* to?" Squeak whimpered.

"Yes, you do!" Bubble barked. Then he took another look at his brother. Squeak really was FILTHY! He tipped some more shampoo into the trough. This time half the bottle went in. "Come on, Mary will be home from school soon," he added.

Slowly, Squeak climbed into the trough. "Ooh! It's fre-e-e-e-zing!" he howled as the cold water touched his tummy.

"Make sure you roll about and get all the dirt off," Bubble yapped.

Shivering, Squeak began to roll about in the water. But, all of a sudden, something happened! Bubbles began to appear. Hundreds and hundreds – and HUNDREDS of them. And they kept on coming.

The bubbles began to cover Squeak completely. "Help!" he spluttered. "Help! There's a Bubble Monster in here, and he's attacking me!"

"Oh no!" Bubble yelped, as Squeak disappeared under a mound of bubbles. "What am I going to do? I've *got* to save Squeak from the Bubble Monster."

Chapter Six

The bubbles in the trough were getting higher and higher, and foamier and foamier all the time.

"Don't worry, Squeak!" Bubble barked. "I'll get help!" He shot away across the farmyard, splashing through all the puddles and the thick mud. He was about to run towards the house. But suddenly he spotted Mary and her mum walking down the lane. Mrs Connor must have gone to meet Mary from school, and they were almost home.

"Mary!" Bubble barked at the top of his voice, sticking his head through the gate. "Mary, come quick! The Bubble Monster's attacking Squeak, and I don't know what to do!"

"Bubble!" Mary ran towards him. "What's the matter? Where's Squeak?"

"Quick!" Bubble danced around Mary's ankles as she came through the gate. "Follow me!" And he dashed back to the stables.

Mary and Mrs Connor followed.

They stopped and stared when they saw the horse trough absolutely overflowing with bubbles. There was so much foam that Squeak was nowhere to be seen.

"What's happened?" Mary asked, looking confused. But just then a little head appeared from the middle of the bubbles.

"Mary!" Squeak whimpered. "Save me!"

"It's Squeak!" Mary cried, and hurried to the rescue. She plunged her arms into the trough, and pulled the little dog out. Squeak was covered in foam and couldn't stop sneezing.

"Squeak, are you all right?" Bubble barked.

Just then, Mr Connor brought one of the horses into the stables. "What on earth's going on here?" he said.

Bubble whined. In his dash to get help for Squeak, he had got rather muddy himself.

Squeak snuggled even closer to Mary and buried his wet, foamy face in her shoulder. They'd had their very last chance now, and Mr Connor would make them live outside in a cold kennel from now on.

"Look!" Mary noticed the bottle of shampoo lying on the ground. "Bubble, were you trying to bath Squeak because he'd got dirty?"

"You're not telling me those pups have been trying to bath

themselves?" Mr Connor said. Then he burst out laughing.

"I think they have!" said Mrs Connor. She was smiling too.

"It's not funny!" Squeak barked crossly, still clinging to Mary. "I was nearly eaten by the Bubble Monster!"

Mary picked up the bottle. "No wonder there were so many bubbles," she grinned. "This is *Extra-Foamy-Kleener-than-Kleen*!"

Her mum and dad laughed even harder.

"I wonder how Squeak managed to get so dirty in the first place," Mary said. Then she spotted something yellow tucked underneath the trough. She put Squeak down and picked it up.

"It's my T-shirt!"

"I hung that out on the line this afternoon," Mrs Connor said. "What's it doing there?"

Mary gasped. "Maybe it blew away and Squeak rescued it!" she said. "That could be why he's dirty! And maybe Bubble got muddy when he ran for help."

"These two are a right pair!" said Mr Connor. He was still roaring with laughter. "You never know what they're going to get up to next!"

Bubble and Squeak's hopes rose. Mr Connor wasn't angry. And Mrs Connor wasn't either. Maybe the pups hadn't lost their last chance after all.

"Dad, Mum, you're not going

to make Bubble and Squeak live outside now, are you?" Mary asked.

Two pairs of big brown eyes stared at Mr and Mrs Connor. Bubble and Squeak waited to hear what they would say.

"Well . . ." Mr Connor looked down at the pups. "I've kind of got used to having them around the house. I think I'd miss them if they lived outside." He looked at Mary's mum.

Mrs Connor thought for a while. "If the pups did come into the house, Mrs Riley would never visit us again," she said. Then she grinned. "But really, I don't care at all! I've had enough of that Mrs Riley's snooty ways!" She turned to Mary. "So as long as Bubble and Squeak stay clean for *most* of the time, they can live inside," she agreed.

"Yes!" Bubble woofed happily. "Squeak, we don't have to live outside in a horrible old kennel!"

"Brilliant!" Squeak barked, and wriggled to be let down.

Mary put Squeak back on the ground, and the two pups raced around in circles, chasing each other's tails. Everything had worked out fine.

"Hey, Squeak!" Bubble playfully nipped his brother's ear and then ran off. "*Kleener-than-Kleen* really does make you SQUEAKY clean then!"

"That's an awful joke, Bubble!"

Squeak woofed, chasing his brother across the farmyard.

"Mind the puddles, boys!" Mary called after them.

Bubble and Squeak had stopped right on the edge of a big puddle of very dirty water.

"Mrs Connor *did* say she didn't mind if we got a *bit* dirty," Bubble woofed, staring at it.

"Shall we?" Squeak barked naughtily.

They both turned round. Mary and her mum and dad were watching.

"We'd better not," Bubble yapped.

"All right then," Squeak barked back. "We'll save it till tomorrow!"